MONICA'S DAUGHTER

MONICA'S DAUGHTER

PATRICIA MURPHY

PARTRIDGE
A Penguin Random House Company

To order additional copies of this book, contact
Toll Free 800 101 2657 (Singapore)
Toll Free 1 800 81 7340 (Malaysia)
orders.singapore@partridgepublishing.com

www.partridgepublishing.com/singapore

This is part 3 of Monica's Outlaws, as you know Monica had a daughter Paula she was sent away to a school for young ladies back east.

Paula was left her grandfathers ranch and now she has come back to run the ranch. Paula did not know much about her mother she was raised by Ethel Carter until she was of an age where she could be sent back east to school.

When Paula got back to her grandfather's ranch William was waiting for her. William put his arms out "welcome back, oh how you have grown" he said with a loving smile.

The author of this book Patricia she did not want to stop at just two books. There had to be a third one. She hopes you will enjoy this one as you did the other two.

Contents

Chapter 1

Learning The Ropes

Paula did not have the first idea about running a horse ranch or any kind of ranch for that matter. When Paula arrived at the ranch William was waiting for her. William's mother was the person that raised her so that would make William her foster brother. "Paula you have grown in to a lovely young lady it is good to have you home. Come give your big brother a big hug" Paula put her arms around him and gave him a big kiss on the check. "It is so nice to be home now let me see how things are." She went inside to see things needed to be done. But to her surprise the house was in very good order there were even a vase of wild flowers on the hall table.

Paula turned to William "Oh William this so nice you did not have to all this trouble for me "Me I did not do this maybe someone else did" "Ah come on who else could have done this "Don't look at me Paula this is a mystery to me". "Well I will take your word for it but I would like to know who did so I can thank them."

Paula walked though the house and could see that someone has been looking after the place. In the kitchen there was food cooking and the table was set for two. "Now I must know who is doing all of this" just then an Indian woman came in. "You are ready to eat now yes?"

she asked "so you did all of this?" "I was sent here to work for you" "oh then what is your name?" "I am call Mar. After they had finished dinner William said that he had to go." Paula get a good night sleep and I will be back in the mornPaula had a bad night all night long she thought she could hear some noises outside. When William came the next day he found her asleep in the big cane chair outside on the porch. He bent down and lightly taped her on the shoulder. "Oh – ah what?" "It is me you were asleep in the chair" "Um yes I had a bad night I keep on hearing noises" She said yawning. I will take a look around and see if I can find out the reasons for the noise"

After William had finishing looking around some men rod up. Paula came out and asked "What do you want here?" Thats okay I will take care of them "William told her." Mister we were told there might be some work out here but if not we will be on our way" "Hey not so fast there is work to be had but first I would like to know your names and where you are from if that is okay with you"? "Um that's fine my name is Frank Dole and the one over there is Clem Watt's the next to you is Brad Camry

The men told William where they had come from and what they can do. They were all showing the bunk house and told what they had to do.

With all that done William told Paula about the men and then the work start. William thought it to be a good idea for him to stay at the ranch for the night. It rained heavy that night and William could not hear any sounds outside.

The next day William thought he would take a quick check of the grounds. That is when he saw two foot prints outside Paula's bedroom window. The prints were small and this told him that it could be a female. He set up a trap so if this person came around again she would be trapped. William had the trap set for day's and not a thing so he left things as they were went about the day to day things.

The ranch was running smoothly a colonel came to see about his horses Paula meet him at the door "hello what can I do for you?" "I am Jim Cooper and I have come to see why we have not got any horses." "Um Colonel do come inside and I will sort this out for you."

Paula show the colonel to a seat "can I get you a drink or something?"

"No thank you I good" "Oh straight down to business I like that"

After their business was over Paula assured him that his horses will be at the fort on time.

After that Paula went to find her grandfathers' books. While she was looking though the house she found an old letter that her mother had written to her. Paula my Dear if you are reading this letter you might think I am dead, but dear you might be surprised. I don't want you to think like that however I will send you a friend and she will tell you all about me.

While Paula was reading the letter William came she put the letter into her pocket. "Paula what did the colonel want"? "Oh nothing much you just forgot to tell me about his order of horses. and while we are on the subject do you have the books for the ranch business."? "They are in the safe the numbers to open the safe is written behind your mothers picture. I only came in to tell you the men and I are going out to bring in some more wild horses. We will be back late to-morrow you will be all right here." Yes... Yes I will be fine I can look after myself" Paula was in a hurry to get him going so she could continue with the letter.

Paula did not know just what to make of the letter she sat in her grandfather's big chair to think. Mare come in and asked "you need to have dinner now it is getting late" "Yes I know Mare did you know my Mother"? Mare stood there thinking of something to say she did not want to tell Paula a lie. "A little miss Paula now how about that dinner"

Paula knew it was not good to push it Paula sat in the living room looking at the letter. Mare saw her and knew that Paula would have a lot of questions. Late that night Paula hear some voices it sounded like to females arguing over something but she could not make out what they were saying. Then there was silence and Paula went back to sleep.

It was late in the afternoon when William and the men got back. Paula was so happy to see them she ran outside to see the horses they got. When she got close to the men she heard Frank say she is nothing like her mother. Clem seen Paula and gave Frank the nudge and they claimed up fast. "You don't have to stop talking just because of me or are you talking about me?" she said with a smile on her face. "No miss Paula were just talking other things. So miss we must get on" Clem and Frank walked towards the bunkhouse.

Later that night at dinner Paula said "William I would like to go to see your mother" "That will be nice she will like that I will have the carriage ready for you." "No I want to ride my horse and go alone you have a lot to do here. I can find my own way there." "Well if you are sure I will have your horse ready in the morning". That night Paula sleeps soundly.

Paula was up early she wanted to get an early start Will had been up since dawn. "You're up Paula your horse is ready. Are sure you don't want me to come with you." William doesn't be a worry wart I will be fine okay"

William left it at that and hoped she would be all right. What concerned was that she was wearing the same outfit that her mother used to wear. But the guns she had strapped on her hips was a nice pear handle not just one but two.

William called Brad to the house "Brad Miss Paula has gone to my mother's place alone. I am worried she might get into some trouble. I want you to follow her but keep out of sight. "I see boss will do" Brad said.

It did not take Brad long before he had Paula in his sight's she was just getting to the boarder. Paula thought this might be a good place to camp for the night. She got a fire going and some food on the go suddenly she hear a noise in the bushes nearby. She swung around and her gun left the holster that fast it was like lighten. A bullet found Brad's shoulder and he screamed with pain.

Paula went to where she hear a noise and to her surprise she found Brad lying on the ground holding his shoulder. "Brad you fool what is you doing here? Don't tell me William sent you to keep an eye on me. Well lest get you to my fire so I can take care of the shoulder".

Paula had a good look at Brad's shoulder and it did not look all that bad. "Brad you are lucky the bullet went right though I will put a bandage on it and Ethel can look at it when we get there."

Brad was very quite all the way to Ethel's. When they got to Ethel's they were met with a woman with a rifle lucky she was a bad shot. Paula jumped of her horse and quickly got around behind Ethel. Just as well Ethel was all so short sighted. Paula grabbed the rifle "Ethel it is me Paula. Ethel put her arms around Paula "Oh my dear I all most killed you. what sort of getup is that your mother used to dress like that you could be mistaken for her. Oh you did give me a scare and who is that wounded man with you?" "Long story Mar I want you to take a look at him and I will tell you all about it."

Brad was resting in one of the bedrooms Paula told Ethel what had happen. Then she asked Ethel to tell her all she knows about her mother. "OH Paula why do you want to know about your mother now. You never wanted to know before." "I know but I am older now and I want to know what she was like after all she was my mother". "Yes my dear I will tell you all I can remember it was so long ago"

So Ethel and Paula sat down and Ethel told Paula what she wanted her to know.

The next day Brad was well enough to travel with the good-byes said they went. Paula keep on thinking what Ethel told her she was sure that Ethel was leaving something out. all though Paula went there to kill Ethel and brad mess that up for. Paula thought it may have done her a good turn this way she can get Ethel to tell her more later.

When they got back to the ranch William got a shock "What happen to I sent you to protect Paula" "Ah yes you did boss um... maybe Paula can tell you all about it" "with that said Brad headed straight for the bunkhouse." Well my girl you want to fill me in? "Well......" Paula started to go inside "William got very angry he called out "Will somebody tell me what happen" "come on I will tell you as soon as I have a cold drink" Paula came out with some lemonade "here cool of and I will tell you".

William was shocked to hear about how fast Paula was with a gun. He wondered what else she has not told him.

A couple of day later a army Captain and his men came for his horse he was standing at the porch when Paula came from the barn "Hi Captain what can we do for you and your men"? "First the name is Captain Ben Fuller" "Like I said Captain Fuller what can I do for you?" "All business I see well we have come for the army's horses" "Clem" Paula called out very loudly" "Yes Miss Paula" Clem answered, "get your ass over here"

Clem ran over to her "yes Miss" "Get the army's horses ready to go the captain is waiting now Captain Fuller if you will come inside I have some paper for you to sign".

The captain and his men rode off without even a second look. Paula went inside and started throwing things around in a fit of temper. "Hey hey stop that what has got your goat anyway" William asked. "Oh I know the nice young captain go under your skin and you was not nice to him. You only have yourself to blame. Now sit down and cool off you will get another chance but done blow it" "All right Mr Smarty how do you know this?" she asked. "There is a fort dance coming up soon and I thought we might say over at Mar's place and go to the dance. I know I will be going and taking Helen Glover.

William went back to work leaving Paula to think about what he said. Paula thought about it all right this was a good chance to get more out of Ethel. as Ethel home was very close to the fort Paula thought it would be an idea to get to Ethel's about two day before the dance.

Paula went looking for William she found him in the barn feeding the animals "William I think we should get to Mar's place about two early so we can rest up before the dance. "I knew you would come around okay how about we go to-morrow."

The trip was a long one and they were glad to get of the horse and rest with some hot coffee that Ethel had just made fresh. "It is good to see you son but what brings you here?" Paula came over to Ethel put her arms around her and said "Mar we don't need a reason to visited do we?"

"Ah no but it would not have something to do with the dance at the fort now would it." Ethel asked "Well it might have, I thought so son are you taking Helen Glover" "Yes Mar I am going to see her to-morrow" William replied. Paula thought this was her chance to question Ethel.

William had just left for Nancy home so Paula had the day to herself. Paula knew that about ten am Ethel like to have a cup of tea so she fixed it for her and took it to her outside on the porch. There were to cane chairs and a nice cane table with a white lace table cloth on it. Paula put the tray with the tea on it down on the table. "Here you are Mar I remembered you like tea about this time. You never did tell me how come you took to drink tea that is English type of thing." Paula wanted to throw Ethel of the track of why the niceties. "Ah my dear that is a story in its self I must tell one day."

Paula did not really want to know she was only after more about her mother. "Mar can you tell me all you know about my mother I need to know no matter how bad it is. I need to be able to move on with my life I know you can understand that."

Ethel sat there and thought about it for a while "Okay Paula I will tell you all of it. But be warned it is not pretty I only hope you can handle it."

So Ethel sat there and Paula sat long side of her Ethel told Paula all she knew. When she was finished Paula had tears in her eyes. But they were faults she had to pinch herself to make herself cry. Ethel did not see her do that. "There I knew you could not handle it your mother was not a nice person come here my dear" Ether put her arms around Paula and hugged her.

After that Paula took a hankie and wiped her eyes and walked out into the yard. Now Paula made plans when to get rid of the old girl she could not do it before the dance. She had to wait to get a chance while the dance was on so she would not be blamed for it.

Chapter 2

The Dance

Paula was having a cup of coffee on the front porch when the captain rod up. "Captain Fuller what are you doing here?" Paula asked nicely. "Oh I thought you might like to go to the dance to-morrow night at the forte" Paula smiled and said "with you I would love to". "Great I will come by for you about 7.30pm is that okay?" The captain had a very broad smile on his face.

William came out and asked "who was that Paula?" "Oh just someone that wanted to take me to the dance. "William bent down and patted her on the shoulder. Later that day Ethel was getting her dress and one for Paula ready for the dance when Paula came. "Mar I Um....don't have a nice dress to were to the dance now I can't go in my old things" "don't worry pet I have thought of that. I got this dress for you a long time ago for you to wear at your end of school party but you never wore it. You just came straight home instead so now you can wear to the dance." "Oh Mar you think of everything."

Ever thing was buzzing with people going and coming and in all of that they were trying to get ready for the dance.

Paula was so excited she could hardly wait she even forgot all about killing Ethel.

The captain turned up to take Paula to the dance right on time. Paula came down the stairs looking every bit a princess Ben was beside himself. All he could say was wow. Ben gave her a corsage for her to wear on her dress "Oh Ben it is lovely and don't you look handsome in your dress uniform."

When Paula and Ben walked into the dance all heads did turn then whispering started among the ladies *"she is the spitting image of her mother hope she will not turn out like her"* one of the ladies said. there was a lot of wisping like that some of it got back to Ethel. William could see that his mother was upset "Mar you look angry what is the matter"? "nothing son you take Helen and have some fun I will be all right" "Well if you are sure" "Yes yes I am fine now scoot"

Paula and Ben were taking a walk outside and it seems to be the same for other young couples. Fay and Sam were out next to the stables and were talking "Sam did you hear what Mrs Cooper was saying about Paula " That was when William and Nancy walked by and heard her "what did Mrs Cooper say"? As they seen that it was William they started to leave "Sam I asked you what did Mrs Cooper say?" "Let it go William it was nothing but idle gossip "William was not going to let it go he knew that his mother was angry at something and this was what it was.

William grabbed hold of Sam's coat sleave "No I want you to tell me what was said" "If you must know it was said that Paula was just like her mother" Sam told him. But of cause they got it all wrong, they did not have all of the facts "Sam you had better set this right Paula is nothing like her mother you tell them Sam "Yeah sure William I will you can count on that"

It was time for supper all the ladies put up a plate of food and drinks. That is soft drink or coffee. But there is all ways someone that puts liquor in to the punch bowl. The ladies were all standing around the supper table talking. One lady said "O yes I heard that too well they say the apple does not fall far from the tree". They did not see Paula standing on the other side of the table. It did not take much for her to work out who they were talking about. Paula went around to the ladies side of the table and face them" "Ladies and I use that term lightly it is not nice to talk about people like that when you don't even know them." With that she walked away and found Ethel "Mar I have had enough I am going to ask Ben to take me home." "Why dear what has happen I thought you were having a good time" "Yes well the good time stoped when I heard some of the ladies talking."

Ethel went to William and told him what was going on and this made him very angry. "Sam Butler you me now" he called out then it started the fight was on the ladies all went outside until it was all over but it took a long time. Then there was a loud scream if came from one of the ladies outside. It was Fay she had been stabbed in the heart it did not take but a minute and she was dead. Paula and Ben were all most out the fort gate when they heard the scream and went back.

One woman called out there it has started there she is and pointed to Paula she did it she did it. Ben stood up in buggy and shouted not she did not we were on our way home when we heard the scream Paula could not have done it. Paula asked Ben to take her home she did not want to around them anymore

The colonel of the forte said, "we had better call it a night so we can find out who killed Miss Fay". Everyone turned and looked at the person nearest to them. then someone seen a dark shadow of someone running to the back of some buildings "There he is going around that building". They gave chase but lost the person in the dark.

Fay's body was taken in to the hall and that is when they saw the knife it was unusual. Ethel said "I have seen a knife like that before it belong to…." As she was about to how a shot rang out from a window the bullet got Ethel in the arm. The army doctor looked at her arm lucky it is only a graze it will heal up mighty quick.

Ben had gotten Paula back to Ethel house safely "Paula I would like to call on you again" "Oh Ben yes I would like that but right now I think I should go to bed I am very tired thank you I had a very good time up to a point" Paula was asleep when William and his mother got home. It was very late when William got back from taking Helen home.

In the morning everyone was up except Ethel she was still in bed. Paula knocked on her bedroom door "come in" "Um Mar are you all right as you were not up as usual I thought there was something wrong with you. Are you sick can I do anything for you?" "No dear I am fine" Ethel did not want Paula to know she was shot last night. Paula bent down to say good bye as they were leaving to get back to the ranch. When she touched Ethel on the shoulder she moaned "what is wrong with your arm" "It is nothing really" "nothing I don't think so" Paula moved the bed cover back then she saw the bandage "I was shot last night it is only a graze it will be better soon. The army doctor looked at it." "Then I will stay and look after you" That won't be necessary I will be able to look after myself you have the ranch to run" "William can take care of that for me I am staying and that is that."

Paula stayed to take care of Ethel she put the plan to kill her to the back of her mind for now.

Captain Ben Fuller came to Ethel's house to see if she was okay he heard all about the trouble they had after they left. He saw Paula sitting under a big old tree reading a book. "Hi you stayed how is Ethel?" Ben asked taken her by surprise "Oh you startled me yes someone had to look after Mar". Paula put the paper away that she was reading into her pocket. She did not want him to see what they were if thought it was a book then well and good.

Ben was happy that Paula stayed now he could get to know her better. "I must get back I have to give Mar her medicine" "I will walk with you" Ben took Paula by the arm.

Paula loved the attention she was getting from Ben and was torn between her good side and her evil side.

Ben came to see Paula every chance he got he did not want her to leave. There was picnic near the lake horseback riding and just sitting and talking. Paula was so happy she did not want it to end but she had to get back to her ranch. It had been a week and Ethel was a lot better now she was doing most of things for herself.

While Ben and her were sitting on the porch she said "Ben my dear I will have to go home soon and it will be a long time before we see each other again" "I knew this day would come but I did want it to. I was hoping you would say" Before he could get an answer a soldier came riding up fast "captain you are needed at the forte A.S.A.P. he turned to Paula "Please say you will wait till I can get back" "Yes Ben I will no matter how long it takes".

Paula sat around thinking about the dance and how nice it was and all the time she had with Ben. William took some time off so he could go and see his mother and Paula. It had been three days since Ben had left and Paula was getting worried. It was good to see William again. When William could see that his mother was all better now he wondered when Paula was coming home.

That night at dinner William asked "Paula when are you coming back to the ranch?" Paula just sat there poking at her food as if she did not hear him. "Paula William spoke to you dear Ethel said and still no response "Don't worry mum I will talk to her later." "Yes son I think she is pinning for Ben he has been gone a long time" "Yes I heard the Indians were acting up again" William left it at that for the night.

The next day William left for the ranch and Paula stayed behind. Paula went for a ride on her own she knew it was still too dangerous to go too far. That is what she thought having not heard anything to say it was allright. William was okay he had to go the other direction away from the fighting. When Paula got back from her ride she could see Ethel waiting on the front porch and knew she had bad news. Ethel walked out to Paula and put her arm around Paula's shoulders "I am sorry but Ben was killed fighting the Indians. They could not send a message until now."

Come inside we will have a drink this is one of the times when we need a strong one. Ethel unlocked the cabinet that had the liquor in it and poured out a large brandy for both of them.

This did not help Paula much it just made her angry and the evil side to get stronger. Her world had just came crashing down and she want justice. It was too late to go back to the ranch now but the next day she was up and ready to go. "Mar I am going home to-day you will cope on your own now that you are better". "That is fine dear maybe you will get some peace working on the ranch" Ethel said.

With all the fun and dancing all over it was time to get back to the real life for Paula.

Chapter 3

Back At The Ranch

The new day brought a lot of work and Paula was going to go out with the men to round up more horses. William objected strongly but that did no good she was going and that was that. Rounding up horses was no walk in the park there were sleeping out on the ground in all kinds of weather. William felt sure she would not last and would want to come home. But he was mistaken she work just as hard as the men no matter what job she was given to do.

Been out there with the men gave Paula a good idea of what it was like. Living ruff like that she got to know the men better she all so found out a lot of things. Like who to trust and who not to trust. Paula was sitting with the men having some dinner and Frank asked "Paula do you want to play some cards the nights get awful long some times."? "Hey that sounds like a good idea yeah" It did not take her long to learn how to play and soon she was winning all the hands. The men did not like this at all Brad was a sore loser "hey who taught her to play"? All the men looked at Frank "Yeah that would be right he cheats" Clem said. "Now boys I don't be like that she is just a good player that all I am losing too.

William thought it would be best if the game broke up "come on men we have a early start best get some sack time okay"

The early start came soon enough everyone was up feed and had the horses on the move back to the ranch.

When they did get back to the ranch everyone was looking for a bath and a good night sleep. Mare had the bath all ready for Paula "you come Misses have a good hot bath some food and to bed. Yes" "Yes Mare I am all done in and looking forward to a nice soft bed. You no tell men yes" "Yes Misses"

After dinner Paula headed straight for her room and on the bed was a note. The note just said don't tell anyone but you are been watched not to harm you but to protected you. "Mare come here Mare" Paula called out. Mare came running down the hallway "Yes Misses I come what is it" "did you see anyone hanging around the house?" "No Miss Paula no one come here" Mare said. Then how did this get here she held note out for Mare to see.?' Not know Miss I not see anyone". Paula knew it was a wast of time asking Mare she would not say anyway. That night Paula was so tied she sleep soundly.

When she woke up there was a dagger stuck in her other pillow next to her. The dagger had the letter S and some fancy writing on the blade. And another note telling her to go to the south of the ranch where she will fined a large oak tree.

Paula did not know if she to tell William or not all morning she pondered over it then thought it maybe better not to. She rode out to where she was told to go and waited. It was not long before someone came the rider was dress all in black. "Are you Paula?" the stranger asked "Yes I am who are you "That dose not matter the point is do you want to hear about your mother or not"? Paula got excited "Yes

I do very much please" The stranger got down of her horse and sat down. Paula sat down next to her.

They talked for a long time and then the stranger said "You can you trust the three new work men they work for me. Let them know you have spoken to Shana. They will then tell you what is to happen I have to go now."

There was a lot for Paula to take in so she went back to the ranch to think about it. She went to the bunkhouse to talk to the men but all the other men were there too. "you three come with me" she pointed to Clem Frank and Brad. They went around the back of the house where nobody could hear them. "I want to tell you that I spoke to Shana. You have something to tell me?" Frank said "Yes you are to kill Ethel and William but not right away you must leave William to last and he must see his mother die. But you must set up an alibi to they cannot blame you are you up for it?" Yes Frank I can do this. Now you all must get back before you are miss I will be in touch."

This was at all order but one she was ready for. That night she stage a screaming act so that William would come in to comfort her. "Now...now it is all right what got you so frighten" "Out.....there a shadow there is someone out there." "I will have a look around" William went out to have a good look around when he came back Paula was fast asleep.

The next Paula told William she was going to spend some time with Nancy near the forte and that she would take Clem with her for support. Ethel house was on the way. "You know this could be a very good idea Nancy will help you get over your fear of living here."

Ethel was having a nap in her cane chair on the porch when Paula and Clem rode up. Paula had along thin dagger she always keep hidden in a pouch on her waist. She had the dagger out and in

Ethel's neck so fast she never even had to get down from her horse. The blood poured out every where and when it was done Paula took the knife out. She found a sharp piece of cane sticking out of the chair. So Paula pushed Ethel's neck on to the cane.

Now it was on to Helen's home for a few days rest. Clem was so surprised at how fast Paula was with the dagger and how so cold hearted she was.

When they got to Helen place Nancy was so surprise she had tears in her eyes "Oh you are not going to cry are you" Paula asked as she gave Helen a big hug "I am just so happy to see you and may I ask what are you doing way out here.?" William thought it would be a good idea I have been having nightmares. Paula hug Helen again. "understandable that ranch was your grandfathers and you have not had time to grieve." William was right you do now about there's things"

Helen made them feel welcome, Paula sleep like a baby and woke feeling good. Nancy asked Paula to go riding with so they could talk.

Clem stayed behind this was the opportunity to search Helen's house he did not know what he would find. Maybe he would fine something to tell him what kind of person Helen was or maybe hiding. He knew there was something but he could not put his finger on it.

Then just before they came back he found it a letter from Chad it seems that he is Helen brother. There was no talk of this before but why. Clem got the letter back where he found it just in the nick of time.

Clem had to get to Paula to tell her just what he had found. That time came when Helen went out to the barn to make sure the horses were watered and feed. "Paula I have something to tell you." Clem said "What you have been snooping again and what did you find this time.?" Paula asked "Oh nothing much just that Helen is Chad's sister. But the burning question is why have no one ever said anything before this" "I am sure there is a very good reason when we go for our ride to-morrow you have a look around and see what else you can find about her."

Chad thought it was time him and William went fishing again after all he might become his brother in law one day. So Chad rode out to see him at his mothers home. But when he got there he got a shock Ethel was still sitting in the cane chair. She was dead and all stiff it looks like she had been there for day's. Chad took Ethel's body into town to the undertaker's then set of for Helen'shome. From town to Helen's was a very long way and it took most of the day and some of the next day it was raining when he got there. Pula seen him coming and had the door open for him "Chad come in out of that rain come near the fire and get warm" "thank you Paula where is Nancy?" he asked Helen came as he said that "Here I am what it the trouble you did not come all this way just for a visit did you?"

Chad sat down at the table "a cup of coffee would be nice" He said It had stopped raining and Paula and Clem made themself scarce but not too far away that they could not ears drop on what was said inside. "Chad what is wrong you are scaring me" "I did not want to say this in front of Paula but Ethel is dead it looks like an accident she must have nodded of to sleep in that cane chair of hers and a piece of the cane pierced her neck she bleed to death." "Oh how awful you want me to tell Paula for you?" "would you I don't think I could do it myself thank you. Now I have to get back to town and file a report. I will come and visit another day sis"

Nancy took Paula for a walk around the place "Helen why have you taken me out here have you got something on your mind?" "Well....

Paula I have something I want to tell you. It is Ethel she is dead I am afraid" "Oh no what happen how did she die" Paula started to cry.

While Helen was telling Paula all about Ethel Clem was looking though Nancy's bedroom. He found an envelope that was hidden stuck on the bottom of a draw. After he had finished reading all the paper that were in the envelope he put everything back the same way as they were.

Paula and Nancy came back inside Clem was sitting in a gig chair near the window having a smoke. He looked at Paula and did not say anything he did not have to the look on his face said it all.

Later that night Clem had a chance to talk to Paula they went out by the barn "Okay what did you fined out. I know you did and by the look on your face it is something big." "Yes I did and yes it is big and juice you see it seem that our Miss Helen is not as clean as she would have people think she is." Just then they we interrupted one of the ranch hands came by so they went back inside but Paula was anxious to find out what Clem knew but it will have to wait.

For the next few days that they were there Paula seemed to be on the mend. As far as Helen was concern. Little did she know that Paula was never ill at all. Paula went out to the corral fence that is where she seen Nancy "Helen I will be going home early in the morning I feel a lot better now thanks for your help." Ah it was nothing you did most of it yourself, you do look a lot better then what you did when you came here.

The next day Paula and Clem were up before everyone else they wanted to get going as soon as they could. It did not take them long to say there goodbyes and they were on their way.

Paula was happy they were away from Helen's place "Now Clem you can tell me all about Helen's background" Oh yes well she own a cathouse and had some ladies working for her. One day a cowboy wondered in looking for some work he did not know what kind of house it was. One woman stated to make friends with this young man and toll him what the ladies do. Maybe she hope she would get him to go up stairs with her. Well she did andHelen saw them and did not like it not one bit.

She knew she was not going to get her cut out of this and her best girl would end up going away with this young man. So she had to put a stop to she shot the young man when he was outside chopping wood for." "phew that is one bad woman so what did they do about it nobody ever heard of it" "I am coming to that Chad covered it up he got rid of the body and then closed her down" "Oh my god this is one big scandal we must keep this to our self agree" Then you might want this". He handed her Helen's diary.

Paula and Clem were all most at her ranch so she tucked the book in to her saddle bag.

There did not seem to be anyone around when they got back. But what they did not know was that William had arranged a surprise welcome home party for them. When they entered the into the house every one shouted welcome home. It was obesely that William had not got the bad news as yet. She took great pleasure in having to be the one to tell him. Now was as good as anyHe got William away from the party "Um I have something to tell you and you are not going to like what it is. Your mother has died Chad found her in her cane chair. It seems her neck got caught on a piece of cane and she bleed to death. I am sorry to have to be the one to tell you we are all going to miss her."

William did not say anything just walked away Paula went in to the party to thank everyone for putting the party on "Friends I don't want to spoil the party but it was a nice idea but we have just got some bad news William's Mother had died. So if you don't mind we will end the party thank you"

After awhile William came back to the house "Paula I am going to arrange mother's funeral I will be away for awhile I will send word so you can come."

Paula told Clem to get Frank and Brad to come to the house I want to talk to all of you. "Guys now that William has left I want all of you to move in here. This ranch has been running on empty for a long time now and we must get some cash flow going are you up for it?" "Oh hell yes" they all agreed. "Okay now down to business I have a very good plan that will net us a large sum." Paula told the men what she wanted them to do and just what was going to happen to get this large sum. In the meantime everything had to go on as usual.

They all turned up at the funeral Paula had to put on the sad look for William and stand by him. When Paula seen Helen she could not see her in the same light as she did before.

At the wake Helen said to Paula "I am sorry for your loss Ethel was like a mother to you she raised you from a very early age." "Thank you Helen yes she was my foster Mother and I will miss her very much."

It was hard for Paula to maintain the pretending as soon as they we all on their way home she was glad to get back to herself.

Chapter 4

Blackmail

Now it was time to put their plan in to action and to the hell with it all. Paula let things quite down for a few days and then it all started.

The usual ranch hands were sent out to get more horses so they would be away for a week at least.

When Paula and the men got to Helen's home they saw William's horse tied up at the front of the house. So Paula told them to go around the back until she needs them. Paula was just getting down of her horse when William came out "Paula what are you doing here"? he asked "I went to your mothers and you were not there so thought you might be here I wanted to know how you were coping. But I see you are in good hands are you leaving then? "Yes I am having mother's house put up for sale and I am going to live with Helen. But not before we get married". "Oh I hope you and Nancy will be very happy"

Just the Helen came out "I thought I heard voices Paula how are you? William you won't be to long I hope" "No I will be back as soon as I can" "Paula come in and have some coffee I just made some"

Paula grabbed the book from her saddle bag and went inside.

The men found a shady tree to sit under and wait. While Helen was getting the coffee Paula put the book on the table next to her. Helen came back to the table with the coffee. Then she saw the book "My diary where did you get it?" "Right now that is not important is important is what is written in it. Wow you have been a very busy woman how would it look if William knew about it. Better still the town found out about you and what Chad did."

Helen was num she did not know what to say "Please Paula give the book and forget what you read Please I am begging you." "Well now that won't do you see I need something from you" "yes anything you say" "this is a big one I know you keep a lot of money here your ranch is doing so well better than mine. So that is what I want all the money you have for now. And if you tell anyone about this I will send this book to the good people of the town.

Helen hurried to get the money "Here I did not think you were like this Paula you are your mother daughter" Helen handed Paula the money. "Yeah yeah stop wining you had better get use to it this is only the down payment. With that Paula left Helen wondering what was next.

Paula and the men rode all night to get back to the ranch. After all they had been thought it was time to celebrate. And celebrate they did well into the early hours of the next day. When it came daylight Frank woke up he was asleep on the kitchen floor. Paula made it to bed and she got up next Clem and Brad were out old on the front porch.

Mare started to make a lot noise in the kitchen getting breakfast. Everyone were walking around like their heads was going to fall off. All day they did not do a thing just lay about the house.

Paula made an attempt to do something she was going to take a ride to clear her head. She was on her way to the barn and that is when she saw two Indian Braves carrying so sacks of flower. They put them on a horse and rode off. "MARE come out here" Paula yelled very loudly. Mare came running "Yes Miss Paula I am here" "Please explain why I just seen to Braves taking some goods from the storage shed" "Yes Miss your mother she said a long time ago that it was all right". "Well that was then it is not all right now you tell the braves to not to come here anymore." "Okay if you say so Iwill but they no like it and it will start big trouble" "I don't care just do it"

After a bad start to the day Paula just had to go for a ride she went to her favourite spot near the river. Paula only stayed for a bit and this time just to clear her head and then she went back she a job for Brad to do.

Brad was sitting up holding his head "Oh that was some party oh my head" "Brad get your ass up I have a job for you" Paula called out to him from her horse. Then she jumped of the horse and poked him with her ridding crop "Come on you are the fire expert I want you to take those old Indian things you know what ones I mean and set fire to Ethel's house so William cannot sell. Make dam sure it looks like the Indians did it"

Paula went inside "Mare where is that coffee I can use it now". With Paula in a bad mode Clem and Frank made themself scares they went to the bunk house for a while.

When brad returned he went straight to Paula "It is done there is nothing but ashes and panty of evidence to tell how did it." Paula was happy, the next thing was to send a message to Helen for money. She also was not going to stop there she want the men to take Helen's prize bull and hold it for ransom. This time she sent Frank and Clem.

Paula was so busy with other things she had forgotten about the men she sent out to get some horses.

Brad came in and asked "Paula don't you think the men should be back with the horses by now?" "Holly cow I forgot all about them I suppose we must go and find what happen to them. Before they could get started a dark figure appeared at the door way. It was Shana "You lost some men and horses I believe?" "yes and what do you know about it?" Paula asked Shana walked around the room then sat in the big chair near the window.

"Well my dear I know a lot of things and you keep going the way you are and you will be dead meat." "I suppose you are going to tell just how I am to run my business. No thanks I don't take orders from anyone". Shana stood up and was about to leave when she said "so be it" then she left.

With all of what Shana had told her Paula found it hard to sleep that night. The next day Paula set things going they had to get out there and find those men. Paula and Brad went to where they thought the men would find horse's. There was no sign of the horses or the men there was only a cold camp fire They searched every where they thought they might be but they did not find them. "Paula maybe that Shana person knows where they are" Brad inquired. "Yes Brad maybe she dose I don't know all I know is that they have gone and I am not wasting any more time on them."

Paula turned around and headed back to the ranch Brad did not like leaving the men out there. But He did not have any say in the matter.

When they got back to the ranch Frank and Clem had gotten back with the bull. Paula had to find a place to hide the bull in case they came snooping around. There was an old supply hut at the back of the house that had to empty for years. As there was a lot of over grown vines and other plant life there it was hard to see the hut. After they had the bull safely tucked away Frank gave Paula a small bag. The bag contain some money and a note that read you bastard will get no more money out of me. And I know you have my prize bull I want him back.

Paula stood there and had a good laugh "Oh my she want s her bull back. She will get it back when I get what I want."

William knew that Nancy had some trouble but he could not get her to tell him what it was. "Helen I know I can help you if you would let me know just what it troubling you." "Dont be silly there nothing troubling me "Helen said looking away from William. That night William could here Helen crying from his bedroom. He went to her and said "That is enough now I want to know all that is troubling you and do not tell me it is nothing" "Your right William there is something it is my prize bull he is missing and I got a ransom note demanding Money for him or they will kill him."

"Oh honey you should have told me when it happen but don't worry I will get him back." That seem to settle Helen down for the night now William had to figure out how he was going to keep to his word.

The next day William was out looking for sign's to see if he could track the bull down. There was only some deep hove prints in some mud that had dried up. While William was out looking for the bull he thought he would call in at Paula's Ranch to see how it was going.

The bull had kicked the old door down on the hut and when to the paddock where there were some cow's. This is where William found him 'William went to talk to Paula and ask her how didHelen's bull get here." Paula how did that bull get in with the cows? That is Helen'sBull. Paula was busy with feeding the other animals. "I don't know what bull we don't have a bull". Paula walked out to the paddock and there was the bull. "William I have not got the faintest idea how it got there. You can just get it out of there and take it back to Helen".

William took the bull back to Nancy and all the way back he could not stop thinking that Paula lied to him. He could not be sure but he had the feeling that Helen knew more than she was saying. He wanted to get to the bottom of thing before it all got out of hand.

William was becoming a thorn in Paula side he had to go but she wanted to do it herself and with Helen watching but how she had to think on this one. Shana appeared at the door way "Paula I have a message for you" Paula stepped backwards she was taken by surprise "What the hell you again Okay what is the message and who the hell keeps on sending me these messages?" "You will know that when time is right. Now it is time to get Helen and William out of your life so we can move on to other things" "Dont you think I know this all ready I am not dumb. Now get lost I don't need to be told what to do". Just as Shana appeared she disappeared

Paula was pacing up and down the room when Frank came in. "Hey leave some rug there. What has got you in lather like that?" "That Shana she comes and goes as she pleases and give me orders." Maybe if you do what she tells you is the only way to handle things. It seem so me she has been at this a lot longer then you have no offence. Frank told her "That is all there is none taken. You may be right I could be looking at this all wrong.

Helen was having her annual get together some of the ladies come over to work on a quilt. This time Paula was asked this gave an idea of how she was going to kill two birds with one stone so to speck.

All the ladies turned up on time Paula came along a bit late. HelenMy dear are you up to this. I hear about the trouble you have been having of late" "Paula nice to see you again I am fine I have no more problems. My dear William has taken care of them for me, thank you for asking then. The Ladies started to work on the quilt and the men were outside looking after the animals. William cornered Frank in the barn "Frank how is everything at the ranch any of your cattle in the family way yet" William was bating Frank hoping he would let something slip but he was to cunning "Well funny you said that I thing a few of them are. Why do you ask?" "Just that Helen's bull got lose and I found it in the paddock with your cattle" "oh you thing he is the daddy of any calves that may come along I don't think so you know we do have some bulls of our own." William did not want to push it any further so he leaf it at that.

The day was along one and it was time for the ladies to have a tea break. Paula when into the kitchen to help with the tea. All the ladies were enjoying the tea break. Paula poured a cup for Helen but they did not see her put something in Helen's cup they were looking at something outside.

Helen got a cup for William "Oh dear the pot is empty I will make another one" "here I will get Frank said I would like one two if that is okay" he did the same as Paula put something in Williams tea.

After the tea break they all went back to the quilt except Helen. "Oh my god what has happen toHelen she is not moving" One woman call out. Then Frank called out "William has passed out on the porch someone send for the doctor" Molly an older lady checkedHelen and then said "don't worry about the doctor send for the sheriff Helen is dead". That started the other women "We are all going to die" One said "We all had tea the same as the both of them" Another one screamed. Molly said "Oh stop your yelling if you were going to die you would have by now. What ever happen it happen very quickly. I think we should say calm until the sheriff gets here."

Everyone was sitting around waiting for Chad to come and they were getting very nervous. At last Chad walked in "what has happen here"? Molly took him to a bedroom where they put William andHelen "We were having tea and then Helen just died then William died we don't know what happen we all had the same and we are all right. We don't even fell a bit sick". "Okay Molly I will take it from here and you can tell the others that they can go home. "I will have the body's taken to town and see what the doctor can tell me".

Chapter 5

True Colours

Paula and her men returned to the ranch and there was someone in the house waiting for her return. Paula sent Frank and Clem around the back Brad and her went inside "Oh it is only you Shana I might have known "You are all ways here" "Yes if call of your dogs I have a surprise for" Paula told Brad to tell Frank and Clem to stand down. That is when Monica walked in she could not walk without a cane but she was alive "Mother you are all right everyone told me you died" "come give your old mother a hug then we will talk." Shana went outside to let them talk.

And talk they did for a very long time "Paula you did everything I asked you to do. Now it is time we made use of those three good men you have out there." Monica got up and walked to the door and summed Shana.

Monica wanted to get her plan in to action she want Paula's Ranch to be their cover as far as people would think she could not do any wrong. So Shana and the men did what was asked of them.

There was a cattle drive to start from town soon and Monica wanted the cattle she had a buyer all lined up. So as soon as the cattle go so far it was time for Shana and the men to do what they enjoy doing. Jake was in charge of the drive he also had some cattle in the heard to. Shana knew it was not going to be easy but they had to get Jake out of the way first.

Along the trail everything was going really good but Jake knew it could go wrong at any given time. Late that night Jake was on watch but he was riding at the back of the heard on his own that is when Clem got him he slipped up behind him and not making any noise he grabbed Jake from behind and slipped a bag over his head. Then knocked him out cold with the butt of his gun. Clem also took Jakes gun of him.

Now that Jake was out cold and the most of the men were a sleep they started the heard moving. With their guns blasting away it did not take long before they started a stampede. Shana had everything under control she was ahead of the heard and when they were far away from Jakes men she slow them up to a walk.

Frank and Brad got them self up to Shana to give her some help while Clem brought up the rear.

After a while Jake got himself out of the bag and rounded up what was left of his men. There was nothing to do but go back to town and get some help. Some of his men were banged up pretty badly. Jake saw Chad standing outside the doctors office "Hey pal what are you doing here?" Jake asked. "Meet me over at the office and I will tell you all about it.

When Chad got all the info he needed he went to tell Jake all about it. "Jake I don't like the looks of this at all it shaping up to be the same trouble we had with Monica. but we saw her body along with Shana's go down the river. They could not have serviced that fall." What has happen here? I know my cattle was stolen by Indians maybe they are doing everything else. "It is though she was a live Helen Glover and William have be poisoned Ethel died and her house has been burnt to the ground it has all the signs of Indians doing it. I don't know just what to make of it Maybe Paula was just like her mother after all." Chad paced around the office things were getting to him. "Ah come on pal we have been in worsted shape then this and we come though it ad we will again. Say Pal I will stay and lend you a hand we can do this"

At the Indian village the chief got the word that they were been blamed for all that was happing around the place and he did not like it. So he thought it was time to fight back.

Paula was in the barn when a horse came in with a rider but the rider was dead and tied to the horse. He had a note on him we no did what they say now you will pay we have your horses and the men have all been killed. Paula showed this to her mother "Well at least we know what happen to the men and horses. But the trouble is we now have the Indians to worried about. Shana I want you to go to the chief and see what we can do to smooth things over. But if you don't have a chance to get close to the chief don't push it."

When Shana got back to the ranch she had bad news for them "The chief would not even talk to me. He told one of his braves to tell me that he is fighting back and there will be no peace." Monica did not like what she heard but she had to except it and move on.

Chad and Jake made a surprise visited to Paula's they had ask her some questions. As luck would have it Shana saw them ride up she made it in the back door just in time. They had Monica out of there fast on to a horse and up into the hills for now.

Jake and Chad came up to the front door and Paula met them on the porch "Hi guys what brings you all the way out here?" Paula asked.

"We have to ask you some question about Helen and William. Did you know they were planning to get married soon.? Chad asked "Um yes I did hear something about that at the quilting party" Paula replyed then asked them in "Please have a seat and I will get some coffee" "No need for that we are okay"

Chad continue to ask Paula question after question and she never got nervous or wavered at all. Then it was over and the said "Paula thank you have been very helpful but we must go" Jake left first and then Chad he turned and gave a small wave.

Chad and Jake were still now further ahead on the way back to town. "Blast that woman she get under my skin for some reason I know she is hiding something." Like what Chad she answered all of you questions?" "Yes I know but there is something about her I just cannot put my finger on it". Jake let Chad think about it and the rest of the way back was very quite.

Monica and Shana came back to the ranch" we will have to set guards so we can be warned in plenty of time. I will need that old hut to be fixed up so we can use that but keep the vines and trees as a cover no one need to know that there is a hut there."

Chad and Jake were sitting in the office when an arrow came though the window and landed in the wall behind Chad. "Bloody hell that was close" Chad yelled. There was a note tied to it "Indians not do what you say they do" Chad handed the bit of paper to Jake "What do you think of this pal?" Chad asked. I think it is time we had a chat with the chief". Jake replied.

Paula had to go into town after she had just got over the boarder a few miles she seen Chad and Jake. "Hi you guys where are you off to ask some more questions?" She smiled. Chad just stared at her and said nothing "something like that Jake answered. Paula knew she got the old shoulder so she rode on.

In town was in the store getting some supplies for the ranch when she heard some men talking about a shipment of gold been taking from the to the bank in the city. Paula all so heard some ladies talking about her. They were saying that they think that Paula will be just like her mother. "Yeah the apple dose not fall far from the tree" one said. Paula turned towards the woman that said that. She walked right up close to her and then punched her hard in the face "Be very careful who you are talking about"

The woman fell back right in to a pickle barrel and the others just stood there with their mouth wide open. By this time Paula had her wagon loaded up so she left.

Chad and Jake were all most at the Indian camp when some brave came up behind them. Chad felt something very sharp poke him in the side. "Uh I wish they would not do that I don't like those spears" "I don't take to kindly to them myself" Jake said. They thought it was better to just do what they wanted. They were taking to the chiefs tent "Have been expecting you two come we will talk." We know that Monica and that other woman in black are still alive we help them out of the river and make them better." "Yes chief I thought that was the case but could not prove it" Chad told him "Jake said "we will make sure that they get the hang mans rope this time. But you and your braves stay out of it if we need help we send word"

Paula had gotten back to the ranch and told her mother what she had heard. Monica gave orders for Frank and Clem to go into town and see if they can find out more about that gold shipment. It was late at night when the men got back but they were told to wake Monica up if she was asleep when they got in.

As it happen Monica was up waiting for them she wanted to get started. She knew it would take Jake and Cad a few days to get back from the Indian's. Frank and Clem were very lucky they got the info that they want just in time for Monica to set things in motion. Once they found out which way they were going Monica sent Paula out to distract the driver of the wagon. She had lie down on the road and pretend to be out cold. When the wagon stop the other would take over the wagon an d drive of men and all. Paula had to deal with the driver. As soon as he got close she grabbed him and plunged her knife into his neck. He fell over that is where she left him. Paula got her horse that was tied up in the bushes.

The men from the wagon was tied up in the barn Monica had a very good way of tiring men up she sued a wet strip of leather and tie their heads to a pole. She also bound their hands to the pole and if they struggle to get free they would tighten up. As nobody knew about this last capper Monica knew she had time to get in touch with her man to get rid of the gold.

Chad and Jake were not far from the town when they came up to what looked like a log on the road. But when they got close they found that it was the driver of the wagon that was carrying the gold. The driver managed to write in the dirt the word Paula. "I knew it Paula has hooked up with her mother and now it starts all over again" Chad screamed.

Monica was very proud of her daughter she come to be just like mum. Paula was glad to be able to be herself. Everything was going so well Monica felt like her old self again and Shana was happy she did not have to be the messenger any more. Monica's gang was growing now there were three men and three women they thought they would be unstoppable.

Things had slow down so the men looked for other things to do. Clem had little senorita(Rosa) he has been seeing so he went to see her. Frank to be on his own so when and sat guard he found a very high hill where he could see everyone coming and going. Brad on the other hand he loved the card when things were going his way and if he did not get caught cheating.

Clem knocked on Rosa's door and she came out but she was very sad. "What has got my little flower so unhappy." Clem asked "You and what you do I heard all about the robbery you and your new found friends did." "Ah you have it all wrong it was not us we do not do these things we only raise horses you know this. Ah come on you and are good yes" "If you tell me you did not do this I will forget all about it yes".

But Rosa did not believe him but she did not want to get him mad. Rosa was afraid of what he might do. Brad found a card game in the cantina at the other end of the village.

Chad and Jake just had to get to the bottom of this before it got out of hand again, and that meant going out to see Paula again.

When Chad and Jake got the small village near the Mexico boarder they stopped for rest. That is when Clem saw them he had to get out of there fast. "Um Rosa I must go I will be back when I can" No you stay I will cook for you please stay "I am sorry but I just remembered something I forgot the boss will have my hide if I don't get it done."

Clem slipped out the back way and rode hard to get to the ranch. When Clem got to the ranch there was nobody there. He looked everywhere and the ladies were nowhere to be found so he thought if he could not find them than Chad wont find them.

Chad and Jake went for some food at the cantina and as luck would have it Brad seen them first. He too headed out the back door and on to the ranch. He found Clem sitting on the porch sipping some water out of a dipper near the water barrel they keep near the steps. For the workers. Hey are you going to drink all of the water or can I have some?" "very funny there is plenty in the barrel" Clem said

The both sat on the step and laugh "You seen them too"? Brad asked "Yes and hightailed it back here but the ladies are not here" Clem said. "That is okay I think I know where they are and if they are there they are safe" Brad replied.

Chad and Jake was on their way to the ranch when they got in sight Frank made a noise like an owl. This gave Clem and Brad the heads up.

When Chad and Jake came to the house they could see Clem and Brad sitting on the porch having a smoke. "Hi you two we are looking for the ladies we don't suppose you could go inside and get them?" "No we could not they are not here and before you ask we do not know where they are now clear off" Clem told them. "Okay we will go but we will come back as many times as it takes until we see them." "It is your time you are wasting now bugger of."

The ladies were at their favourite spot and the water look very inviting so Paula striped down to her underwear and went for a cool dip. "Come on you two the water is fine" Paula called out to them. Shana did the same thing. But Monica could only sit at the edge and paddle her feet.

Frank thought it would a good idea to tell the ladies he all so went to the ranch. "Brad do you know where the ladies go?" "Yes I think so" "well go and let them know what to expect and Monica can make up her own mind what to do."

Chapter 6

Laying Low

Brad got to the water hole and the ladies were all enjoying themself so much they did not hear Brad come up on them "Hey ladies your dead where you stand" he called out. Monica turned around sharply "Who the bloody hell is that"? she pulled a gun out from under her skirt and pointed it straight at Brad. No You are dead where you stand Brad you should know better than that never sneak up on anyone" "yes I did not think I came out here to tell you that Chad is at the ranch and you had better go into hiding for a while."

Monica thought of an idea to put Paula back in good face with the law. She told Paula what she wanted her to do. Paula did not like it but could see that it was the only way. Paula found her way back to the old hut without been seen there she dress in one of her old dress and cut her arm her leg put scratches on her face. Then rubbed dirt all over her cloths and to make the cuts and scratches look like it had happen days ago she had to put an old dirty bandage's on them. She all so messed up her hair and put some bit of stick and some leaves in to her hair.

Paula came out to the path near her home and called out help, help, someone help me. Jake ran out of where they were waiting for Paula to get back. When he saw her she fell to the ground. He rushed to her and carried her inside.

Chad and Jake listen to her story of woe but Chad was not convinced. Clem came in and he told them that he would take care of her. Jake looked at Chad and asked "Why do you not believe Paula it could have happen the way she said"? "Yes maybe but it seem a bit to convent for my likings." Chad looked worried. Jake did not push he knew when to just say nothing.

Jake and Chad had been friends for a long time and they have gotten to know each other well. Jake knew that Chad was wrestling with something and it was not what was going on now. Jake had to get him to open up to him so that Chad could get on with the problem at hand.

Later on their way back to town they stopped and made camp this was a good time to talk Chad. "Chad I knew you have other things on your mind. You know you can talk to me and it stays with me." Jake gave Chad time to think about it. Chad knew he had to talk to someone and he knew he could trust a long time friend." Okay Jake what I tell you is just between us right." "Yes it stays with us no matter how bad it is"

Then Chad told Jake all about Nancy been his half sister and that she own a whoa house. He all so told him about getting rid of a dead man from the house. Jake did not like what he had heard but he could understand that Chad was just protecting his family.

Jake reassured Chad that what he told him would go no further "Chad you was only looking out for your sister you must put it behind you. Put the past where it belongs in the past." "Yes I know but I think Paula has found out somehow and I know she will use it against me somehow" Chad leaned forward and held his head in his hands. "Chad now I understand and we will cross that bridge when we come to it together old pal" Jake put his arm across Chad's shoulder.

Monica heard that the law had gone she went back to the house. After every one had settled down it was time to make their next move. This time Monica made sure that they would not be surprised again she had extra men out and around the ranch. To make it look like Paula was okay she had the ranch run the way it should be. There men working with the horses and other men doing other work around the place.

All was quite in town Chad and Jake was sitting in the office trying to work out how to catch all of them. Chad came up with an idea "What do you think of this Jake? I will set a fake wagon of gold and send it out. She will have to go for it. "Mmm maybe but do you think it is too soon for her to fall for that" Jake was not all that sure. Chad thought it was worth a go.

The wagon was set up and sent out but it did not get any takers. So it returned with all on board. Chad went out to the men in the wagon "what happen?" "it was no good it did not work we think she has a spy in town" One of the men told Chad. While Chad was talking to the men on the wagon an old lady walked passed. She was dress all in black and carried a walking stick. No one notice her she just walked to the stables got her buggy and left town.

They did not Know that it was Monica herself. Jake and Chad went back to the office. "Jake I don't mind telling you I am all out of ideas Have you got anything."? Chad asked. "Um I just might have but I will have to think on this for a while" "Anything would be good right now." Chad was desperate he want all of them behind bars again.

While Monica was in town she deposited a large sum of money in Paula's account. She had to do this to make Paula look good in the towns people's eyes.

Things were going very slow so Clem Brad and Frank decided to go fishing. But when they were all most where they wanted to be the weather started to turn bad. It got windy and it started to rain heave "Oh that dose it I am out of here anyone coming"? Clem called it a day "Yes me to" Brad. But Frank was very stubborn he was not going until he caught a fishing.

All this was all well and good but the only thing he caught was himself. A very large tree fell on him. He was knocked out cold but as luck would have it an Indian girl came to his rescue. She managed to get the tree high enough to drag him out. She took him to the Indian village to her tee-pee she was taking care of him. When the chief walked in" you cannot take care of the white eyes they are enemy". "No he is hurt and if I can save him he then belongs to me. You all ways say that is this not true?" "Yes My daughter it is but he is white man. No good for you he is bad medicine he break white man's law" "I don't care I fix him and then we will see".

When Clem and Brad got back to the ranch Monica asked "where have you two been we have work to do. Hang on where is Frank?" she asked. Both of the men turned and looked "ah we left him fishing he said he was not coming back until he caught something." Clem said with a smile. Monica was not happy about this but she knew that she needed all of the men. "Get your sorry asses out there and find him" She started slapping her riding crop on her hand. The men knew they had better make tracks.

But the only place they were going was the bunkhouse it was still raining. There was no way they were going out in that.

Paula watched her mother take over things and she did not like it not one bit.

Paula waited till her mother calmed down then she said "Mother you seem to be taken over my place. have you for gotten I own this ranch now and I give the orders not you." "Paula I have all way been in charge of things around here You have just been doing everything I tell you to do if you think about it. The orders came to though Shana and you did what she told you. You have no idea how to order a gang. So let not have any more of this come on I am doing this for you." Monica put her arms out to Paula and she hugged her tightly.

Frank woke up and the Indian girl said "Ah you are alive you all most died." "Where am I" Frank tried to get up. "no you must stay there you are strong enough to get up yet." Frank laid down again and had a good look around himself. He could see that he was in a tee-pee and a lovely young girl was sitting next to him. This was no good he had to get out of there but fast. He had broken his arm and she strapped it up with some pieces of wood for splints.

The chief came in to see how he was doing "You are better now you must go I will have your horse brought to you and you go." Frank knew he had to leave and so with the help of the Indian girl he got to his feet. He felt a lot of pain from his ribs but he keep on moving to his horse. The chief helped him on to his horse.

Clem and Brad set of to find Frank they got to the river where they last saw Frank. All they could see was his hat and a fallen tree. "It looks like he was hurt and someone save him" Brad said "Yeah but who and where did they take him" They found some horse prints in the dirt so they followed them as far as they could. Suddenly they seen a rider up ahead the rider did not look like he could go much further. So they moved up a bit faster. "It is Frank" Call out Brad got one side of him and Clem the other and walked their horses slowly.

It took some time but they finely got back to the ranch. Monica was at the corral fence checking on some horse that were brought in. After this was still a working ranch." Oh my god take him into the bunk house I will be over there.

At the jail Chad was sitting at his desk trying to think how they could catch Paula and the rest out. Jake came up with an idea "Hey Chad how about I go out to see Paula just as a friend visiting. And that way I can get to talk to me. Jake asked. "Hey that might be a good chance of getting what we want we don't have anything else going for us" Chad was please to see someone was thinking he was all out of thoughts.

Jake was all most to the ranch when a rider came up to him it was the chief. "You are the one they call Jake yes."? "Yes chief I am what do you want?" "I tell you something one of the bad white men was at our camp my daughter found him half dead under a tree. She make him better then I sent him away". "Thank you chief that will make things a bit better I am on my way out there now." Jake said good –bye to the chief and continued on to the ranch.

When he got to the ranch Paula was coming out of the house with an arm full of blankets. "Here let me help you with those" Jake rushed over to help. "Thank you Jake it is very kind of you" Paula said with a smile. Paula walked towards the bunk house Paula took the blankets of Jake and took them inside. Jake did not follow her he thought it would be better if he stayed out.

After a while Paula came out she seen Jake standing near the corral "Um Jake it is all way's nice to see you but what brought way out here".? "I did not thing I needed a reason to visited my friends". "Well no you don't but with all the questions Chad had been asking" "Stop right there young lady but that is Chad's job he has to ask questions". "Oh I guess so hey how would you like to have a cup of coffee and a piece of my famous cake I just made it this morning."

So they were friends again just what Jake wanted so he could ask her anything and get what he wanted to know. While Paula was keeping Jake busy Shana and Monica moved Frank into the old hut. Clem and Brad was working with the horses and everything looked as it should.

Frank was in a bad way Monica thought that one of his ribs may have punctured his lung. He needed a doctor. But Monica did not know a doctor she could trust. "Monica there is an old doctor that lives at the other end of village I think you will be able to trust him. Shana said." Well you get him and if he cannot be trusted you will have to deal with him.

Jake was talking to Paula and having a cup coffee. "Paula if you need to talk to someone please send for me. I must go now I have to get back to my place." "Thank you Jake I will it was nice seeing you again".

Shana had the doctor to Frank fast after he had looked at Frank he said "It is to late there is nothing I can do for him now. You were right the rib did puncture his lung he wont last long sorry." With that Shana took the doctor back and told he had better keep his mouth shut or it will be the last word he will say. "Shana I hope you can trust him he looked at me and he knew who I was" Monica growled.

The older Monica got the more unstable she become and that was dangerous.

Jake made it back to town and when he found Chad he told him "Pal your feeling about Paula is unfounded she is as straight as we are. But I do think she is living with some dangerous people out there and she was afraid to tell me." "What do base that thinking on she not the goodie, goodie you seem to think she is" Chad had gotten hard and bitter in his old age not that they were all that old. Jake did not like the way Chad was talking so he left.

Chad was not happy with the way he treated his best friend he just slumped down into his chair. This were starting to get to him maybe it was time to give up been the law and just retire.

Jake was in his room at the hotel packing to go back to his ranch after all there was nobody to take on his job. He could not leave it all up to his family.

Chad got to the hotel just as Jake was leaving "going somewhere pal please forgive my outburst I think I should get my mouth in gear first then think before I say things" Chad put his hand out to Jake they shook hands "all right but I will help you this time but then I am done. I have a place of my own to run you know" "good man maybe you should bunk down with me in the jail."

Chapter 7

Precious Gems

Mrs Peabody ran a guest house for V I P's and she was getting everything ready for the governor of the state and his wife. That is governor George Greenhill and Hazel Greenhill.

The governor train pulled in to the station and three buggy's was there to meet them. One buggy for the servants and one for the bodyguards and one for the governor. The they took two white stallions of the train they were headed for Paula's Ranch.

Monica was up early and she had everyone else up too." Now as you all know the governor's horses are arriving to-day. We are expect to break them in my father had good name around here for breaking horse. That is why we got the job of doing this. This also act's as a good cover for Paula. Shana and I will be in the old hut if you need us at anytime

Chad was at the guest house to welcome the governor and his wife. Monica sent Clem to check out the governor's quitters and see they were carrying anything of value. Clem found his way up the drain pipe like a rat and in to the hazel's bedroom/sitting room. He searched all around then he found a leather case. When he opened it he could hardly believe his eyes. There were gems of all kinds but he had to close the case in hurry. Hazel's maid was coming he got behind the door.

When she open the door he grabbed her and put his hand over her mouth so she could not scream. "Then whispered in her ear" *If I take my hand away don't scream okay.* She moved her head from side to side then he took his hand away. She was a slim young woman he looked her up and down while he had hold of her. Then he run his hand up to her breast they were small but firm. She did not try to get lose and he continue he then run his hand under her skirt. With one thing and another they found themself on the bed making passionate love for long time.

Later Clem was laying back on his pillow and asked "Oh by the way what is your name?" "My name is Renee I am from France "You wont tell them that I was here will you?" "No of cause not you I like are you going to rob us now" "Ah yes my little one but I will be back for you later.

Clem got the leather case and left the same way he come with a small wave he was gone.

Renee waited for a while and she straighten up the room and then went down stairs screaming "Madam Madam we have been robbed" Hazel went over to her she put her arm around her and then "calm yourself and tell me just what happen." Hazel made Renee sit down so she could calm herself.

While Renee was telling Hazel all about the robbery George came in "what is this a robbery?" He asked. "Yes dear all of my jewellery have been taken." George was angry he when straight to the sheriff's office. "Sheriff you will have to get a possie together my wife's jewellery has been stolen"

Chad got some men together and it looked like he was going out to search the missing gems. Jake on the other hand went straight for Paula's he knew that the gem would end up there. But Monica was one step ahead of them again. She Had Clem meet them at the water fall. Clem gave Monica the leather case and when she opened it and saw all those gem" woe this will take a lot of selling my but they are beautiful.

Chad led the posy on a merry chase he knew that the gem went straight to Monica. When Chad had come in to town looking all dusty and dirty George was waiting for them "Well did you get the blighter"/ "Sorry sir but I think we won't have a chance of getting your gems back" "I think you are a sorry excuse for the law around here." "Yeah well be that as it may this lawman is looking for a bath and a good night sleep."

The governor was not happy with this but there was not much he could do about it.

The next day Chad waited for Jake to return. Paula when to the water fall to tell her mother that they were out looking for the gems. "In that case we had better get rid of them right away." Brad got back with the dealer Monica showed him the gems "Oh my these will fetch a pretty penny now let me see what I can do for you"

Both party's we happy with the deal and the dealer took off he needed to get rid of the gems fast.

Everyone returned back at the ranch Monica wanted to check on Frank she looked at him and he was dead.

Chad was just coming on to the ranch when Monica was just about to go into the house. "That snoopy sheriff is back again we cannot make a move with him hanging around all the time." Monica moaned "Let me take care of him once and for all" Shana said. While they arguing how was going to take Chad out Paula was outside talking to Chad. "Chad how nice it is to see you again. Come have a look at the two of most beautiful horses you have ever seen". She lead him down to the corral "There what did I say?now Chad what was the reason you came here?"

Chad walked back up to the house "There was something I wanted to ask you. Have you seen any strangers around here of late?" "no why"? "there has been a robbery of some jewellery and as you are close to the boarder I though you may have seen some strangers."

Chad thought it was better to leave while he was still had his shirt. But Shana had other ideas she let him get ahead then she follow him. Shana waited till she had a clear shot then she shot him. Chad fell forward on to the horse but keep on going. Shana thought he would not last long so she returned to the old hut. Monica was waiting for to get back "Where the hell have you been.?I don't like my people go off without tell me what they are doing" Monica said Shana did not like tone Monica took so she just walked further into the hut and sat down.

Monica thought it was better to let her have sum space for now. Chad was wounded in the shoulder and he was getting weaker by the minute. The pain was so bad he blacked out and fell to the ground. Some Indian braves found him and took him to the camp. "Oh another hurt white eyes, but this one is lawman". The chief said and told the women to look after him.

Chad came to and looked around he knew he was in the Indian camp. Just then the chief walk in "Ah at last you are better you must rest and the soon you will be able to leave." "How long have I been here chief"?" "Three moons you are a very lucky my braves found you when they did." "Chief will you send word to Jake" Chad asked

Later that day Shana told Monica what she had done "Well Shana I only hope he is dead because if not he will come back looking for the person that shot him." Monica looked every worried. "Dont worry he is dead I seen him fall."

Monica wanted to get rid of the both of them Chad and Jake. So she thought up a plan that would make Jake see red. Jakes wife and children were going to feel the blunt of it all. This time she had enlist the help of Brad and Clem.

As soon as Jake got the message he went straight for the Indian camp. "Hey pal what have you got yourself in to now?" Jake knelled down long side of him and took a look at his wound 'Yeah someone shot me in the shoulder and I think I know how. We will have to be on our guard from now on". I Reckon you are right there come on let me get you up and out of here".

Jake got Chad back to town in to the hotel and sent for the doctor to look him over. Monica made her move she headed for Jakes place to do a lot of harm to jakes family. Brad was the fire bug and Clem like the ladies not that he much of a chance to have some fun with the ladies.

Jake knew there was only one thing to do he had to go back out to Paula's. But htis time he would go in and look around on his own. He would not leave until he had found what he was looking for. Jake came on to the ranch a different way. Paula was at the corral watching them break the white horses.

As Jake was riding to house his horse tripped and redid up and Jake came down with thump "What the hell" then he saw what made the horse trip. It was freshly dug grave. Jake found a sharp stick and started to dig he did not have to dig far. he saw that it was Frank in the dirt. Jake left his horse tied up to a tree and went in on foot.

Coming in the way he did he soon found the hut hidden away from sight. That is if you came from the other way.

One of the men that were breaking the horse went to the bunk house and that is when he saw Jakes horse. It was shear luck that Shana was down at the house.

Monica and her gang had to stop over night it was a long way to Jake's home. They wanted to get to Jake's home when it was early in the morning. Jed came down to Paula at the corral "Miss Paula I seen a rider go into the old hut." "Thank you Jed I will take care of him." She had to change from the dress she had on to something that would not trip if she had to move in a hurry. Paula changed into some jeans and shirt she got her whip and then went to the hut.

Paula was in a mood to do him some serious harm she saw inside with his back to her. She stepped up behind him and wiped the whip around his neck. He grabbed the whip with his hand and tried to get lose but it was of no uses. Paula had quickly got her gun out and knocked him cold. Then she called out Jed "Jed come here I need you".

While Jake was out cold Paula turned him over to see how it was. "Oh Jake you" she said Jed took Jake to the barn and tied him up with the wet leather strips they keep just for this sort of thing. Those that came snooping got the same treatment. One leather strip around the forehead one around the ankles and the other around the wrist which are all tied around a pole in the barn.

Monica and the men got to Jakes ranch just as his wife Millie was milking the cow for the morning breackfast. Monica stood at the back of her "Ah nice fresh milk." Millie got such a fright she jumped up and knock the pail of milk over. "Who are you and what do you want?" "Now is that any way to treat a friend Clem said "You are no friend now leave my property at once" Clem stepped a little close to Millie. She grabbed the pitch fork that was nearby and lunged at Clem. Clem side stepped the fork and got around the back of her. He got hold of her arms and made her drop the fork.

Monica and Brad went over to the house she knew that the children were about to get up soon. Elizabeth and her brother James came into the kitchen "Mar what is for breakfast?" James asked as all boys do.

That is when Elizabeth saw Monica she knew something was wrong. "Where is our mother and what have you done with her"? Monica went to Elizabeth "Now don't you worry your pretty little head about that" James went to go outside but Brad stopped him "Where do you think you are going little man. I thing you had better sit down over there." Brad pointed to a chair at the table.

Clem had Millie striped down to her under wear and she was fast out. He was trying to get her to come to. Clem found a bucket of water then he threw it over face. Millie started to cough and the she sprang to her feet" no don't touch me or I will scream." "ah no not that I hate it when women scream". Clem took the bandana from around his neck. He got hold of Millie again and then he stuffed the bandana in her mouth so she could not scream. Clem tore at her underwear until she had nothing on. He run his hands all over her body and then he had long sex with her.

James slipped out the back door when nobody was watching he then ran to the barn. What James saw there made him sick he had to leave.

Paula walked around the barn waiting for Jake to come around. Jake came around and then he asked "Paula why I just don't understand you was raised in a good family. What happen what went wrong some people were saying that the apple never fell far from the tree. Were they right come on Pauls help me to understand"? Paula looked at Jake "You want me to tell you what went wrong. Well let me see first I was left with some people I hated then I was sent off to school. I never got the chance to get to know my mother. Yes I suppose I am like my mother her blood runs though me so think it was all ways in me to be like her." With all opf that Paula just walked away and left Jake to think about it.

Clem walked to the water barrel and wash the blood of his shirt and hands. Millie had got a hold of Clem knife and stuck it into herself this was the only thing she could do her life was all but over.

James ran back in the back door and told his sister what he saw. This made her cry for a long time. Monica told Brad to get things ready to torch the place. She took the children outside put them on a horse and told them to go to their father. With the children out of the way Brad set fire to the house and the barn. Monica rode off with the men and then she yelled happy days this should have been done a long time ago.

Chapter 8

Betrayed

When Monica got back with the men Paula greeted her with the news that she had Jake in the barn. Shana had left before Monica got back she was headed in to town.

Elizabeth and James made into town they went to the sheriff's office. The deputy told them that their father was not there but they could wait till he got back.

When Shana got to town she found out just where Chad was hold up. She knew that there would be a guard on Chad's door so she had to get him out of the way. Or maybe she could use him as her ticket into Chad's room.

Shana thought it would be better if she came up the back stairs of the hotel. From the door of the back stairs she could see all of the hall way and the guard outside Chad's room.

Monica was very pleased at this news she went out to the barn "Well, well we meet again Jake. Oh you seem to be all tied up" "Monica I thought I would never see you again. Untie me and I will make sure that the law goes easy on you." Jake begged "No. No my friend now your children will know what it is like not to be able to say good by. They will also see what it is like growing up without old mum and dad. This is what you did to me."

Shana came up behind the guard and put her gun to his back and said "now take me into see Chad or your life will be over in a flash." The guard walked slowly into the room with Shana behind him. "Sorry boss she has a gun in my back". "now let me see what do you think I should do with him. I know". Then she took her knife and slit his throat and just threw him out the window over the balcony. She did not take one eye of Chad she quickly turned the gun on him.

Some men came running out to the street to see what had happen. They sent for old doctor Bob but there was nothing he could do for him. Shana knew that there would be a crowd of men up there soon so she said "Just thought you might like to know that Jake wife has been killed and he is tied up in Paula's barn. Believe it or not it is up to you." Then Shana made timely exit the same way she came.

The deputy came running to the hotel up the stairs two by two only to fined that Chad was all right. "Chad Jakes children are in your office they are looking for their dad." "That's okay I will come down and talk to them" "But boss you are hurt you should not be getting up" "I am fine now just get me my trousers."

Clem and Brad were in the bunkhouse playing cards as there was nothing to do. "Hey Brad I have had enough of just sitting around what say we make something happen for our selfs". Clem looked right at Brad "Yeah what do you have in mind."? Brad was interested in what Clem was saying. They did not see Shana standing at the door and she made sure that they would not see her. "Mmm come and I will show you what I have in mind." Shana was fast on her feet she ran down to the corral and she could see them from there.

Elizabeth and James got tied of sitting around so Elizabeth remember that their father told them a long time ago if they find themself in trouble to go the guest house and Mrs Peabody would help them. chad was still hurting but he had to get back to the office to see if what Shana had told him was true. The deputy help him across the street and when they got there the children were not there. Chad flopped down in his chair "well deputy you said there were two children here where are they" "I swear boss they were here they must off left". Chad leaned over his desk and that is when he seen the note that Elizabeth had left. "Elizabeth has her father's brains good girl."

So now he had get down to the guesthouse and talk to the children.

Monica went out to the barn to torment Jake some more "Hi you still hanging around here Ha, Ha, osp you cannot get away can you." Jake did not say anything he just hung there with his head hanging down. "Ah come you really think I am going to fall for that do you?" She went close to him and moved his head up then let it go his head just fell back down.

Monica was convince that he was dead so she cut him down and his body just fell to the floor. She never thought to find out if he was breathing or not. Monica just walked away and never looked back.

Jake waited till he was sure that she was out of sight. He got up slowly he could only move very slow. He got hold of an old pieces of timber that was laying around it help him to walk. No one had thought to take his horse away from where Jake tied it up so it was still standing there.

Chad got to the guest house and asked to see the children. "Now sheriff it is far too late please let them sleep and I will bring them to your office in the morning"

Chad left the guest home and went back to the hotel so he could get a good night sleep.

The next day Mrs Peabody had the children down at the office as she said she would. Chad made the children feel comfortable then he said "Elizabeth you are the oldest I will ask you can you tell me what happen at your ranch."? "cant remember much but when we came down for breakfast there were a man and a lady in the kitchen. I asked where was mum and the lady just made us sit down. James sneaked out the back way and what he saw was not nice. I don't think he wants to talk about it. Elizabeth put her hands up to her face and started to cry. "Thats fine maybe you can tell me this did James tell you what he saw"? "Yes he did but I think I should tell Mrs Peabody" "All right why don't you tell Mrs Peabody and I will talk to her later."

Shana follow Clem and Brad to an old abandon mine they went inside and Shana waited till they came out. "Well now what do we have here? she asked leaning back on the side of the mine entrance and her gun in hand." Oh blast where did you come from? "Clem asked putting the saddle bags down." Tha's the way boys put the bags down they look heavy. Now back off come all the way to me. "When the men go close to her she walked towards the horses and the bags." Now go inside so I can leave go on back into the mine. "Once she had them into the mine she fired a shot into the box of dynamite the whole of the mine caved in on top of them.

After what Mrs Peabody told him he knew what he had to do next. Chad got about half way there and he ran into Jake half dead. "Man you look as good as I feel we are a good pair." Chad got hold of Jakes horse and helped him down of the horse. Chad made Jake as comfortable as he could and then made a fire. "We can rest here for awhile and you can tell me what happen" Chad said "You were right Paula is in it up to her pretty neck" Jake moaned.

After Shana had hidden the bags she went back to the ranch she was not ready to leave just yet. Everyone was at the corral the governor's aid came for the horses. A smartly dress young man he came in a buggy not one for riding a horse it seems. Paula had one of the men tie the horses on the back of the buggy.

Shana knew it was time for her to go there was nothing left for her here., She followed the Aid the two white horses was to bring her a fair prize. Suddenly Paula turned around she thought she heard a horse. "Mar is that Shana up there"? Monica looked up towards the small hill at the back of the house. "My god yes what on earth is she doing up there?". Then they saw the aid and the horses pass by the hill then the penny dropped.

Monica knew then what was about to happen." Shana you bitch leave those horses alone "She called out" but she were too far away for her to hear. "That bitch I will get her for this mark my words she will pay big time."

Shana knew after she got the horses she had better keep going. But she was not messing around this time so she took aim and then shot the aid in the head. He fell straight to the ground. All Shana had to do was go and get the horses.

Jake feel asleep and Chad let him stay there for while the time was getting so Chad thought that it would be better if they both got some rest and started again the next day. Shana had gotten so far and found it was getting dark so she had to stop and camp for the night.

Early the next day Monica and Paula took off to find Shana and get the horses back all so deal with her. Paula wanted to Know just what her mother had in mind for Shana she want to get revenge on her too "Mar when we catch up to Shana what did you have in mind for her?" "Dont you worry she will get what is coming to her I will see to that"

Shana thought she would go a long way out of the area some where she can unload the horses.

Chad and Jake started their journey the both of them had a score to settle. Chad had told him about his wife and children "Sorry about your wife but the children are okay. They are staying with Mrs Peabody for now." Thanks pal I owe you one: Jake said. "No you don't you pulled my fat out of the fire many time."

By the time Chad and Jake got Paula's ranch there was nobody around so they took the chance and made a good search of the place.

Shana had crossed the river and took a sharp turn north she knew a trading place not far from where she was. Monica thought that Shana would go to the Indians but Monica did not want to go there. "Paula I am not welcome in the Indian camp I want you to go and see if Shana had been there." "Well we might have a problem with that to see I am not a friend of the Indian' s nighter. Dont you think we are wasting time out here I think that at some point Shana will come back to the ranch." Paula told her mother. "I am not sure but you could be right." Monica and Paula head back to the ranch the only place they felt safe

After Shana had gotten rid of the horses she thought that she would go back to the ranch and deal with Monica and Paula. She had to do this because she knew that one day they would come after her.

Chad knew that they would come back soon so they had to find a place to hide. So they thought somewhere up high would be good and the small hill at the back of the house was where they sit right behind the big old tree.

Monica wanted to show Paula where her stash was so if anything happen to her Paula would have something to back her up if she need it. But when they got there what Monica saw made her very angry "Bitch Shana did this now I know why we have not seen Clem and Brad. Those two lay about were all way smooching around for something to eat."

A rider was coming onto the ranch and Chad and Jake sit tight and watched. Shana got back to the ranch before Monica and she was able to get her story straight. Nothing was happen for awhile then two more riders came to the ranch it was Monica and Paula "Oh this should be good the three of them all in one go" Chad said Jake put his hand on Chad's shoulder "wait it may be better to see what unfolds I have a feeling the lid is going to blow on this one" Jake sat back down to wait.

Chapter 9

The last days

Jake was right when Monica entered the house she walked straight up to Shana and gave her a right cross "Now bitch tell me what you have been doing" Shana stepped back a pace then with a quick flick of her wrist a knife flew straight for Monica. But she was to quick and doge the knife it stuck in the wall behind Monica. Paula reached up and pulled it out. "If you think I will ever cross you I don't know. I followed Clem and Brad to see just what they were up and if anyone was going to cross you it was those two they knew where you hid your stash so I took it away from them and planted somewhere else." Shana was sitting on the floor with hand up to her face. "Yeah that tell me about my stash but what about the horses?"

Shana stood up and walked to the table with the whisky bottle and glasses were. When she poured herself a drink she said "Yes I took the horses and I sold them and got good money for them. That too is with the rest of your stash" Shana flopped down in to a big chair and drank.

Chad and Jake were sitting on the hill waiting for something big to happen but it did not. The men were still there and it was getting late "I don't think anything is going to happen we might as well get settle in for the night" Chad sad as he made himself comfortable.

There was no movement in the house because there was trap door in the living room floor that Paula had made so if she needed to leave without been seen. Paula had taken them out though a tunnel she had made it took them out to the river. "Paula you are your mother's daughter but there is only one thing you did not think of. Your mother has bad legs and cannot walk far" Shana informed her. "Shana I was not thing of anyone been with me. But there is a canon up a ways it is not far. I have been keeping horses there. I all so thought of some supplies to." Paula snapped at Shana

Chad and Jake woke up the next day "Oh I would kill for a nice soft bed" Jake announced. "I am not worry about that I am going down there. I am not sitting on my hands anymore. Chad started of when they got to the house and went inside they found it empty." Yeah just as I thought they lit out in the night "Chad stomped out. Jake followed him but he tripped on a fold in the rug. After he picked himself up he had the rug in his hand and that is when he saw the trap door." Chad you had better have a look at this. Jake called out to Chad.

Chad came in again "Now what is you would like a nice hot cup of tea or something". Chad asked walking to him.

Jake was in no mood for wise cracks "Stop with the wise cracks take a look for yourself. Jake pointed to the floor. The trap door was set a jar like someone was sending them a message. "Jake we have been led by someone I would like to know which one of them it is" Chad said "I don't know but I am glad someone helping us. We need a break see if it continues." Jake and Chad followed the tunnel and it took them to the same part of the river.

Paula and Shana helped Monica to the cannon and there about five horses in the cannon." Why five horses Paula are expecting company "Monica asked Mar I did not think we would be two down okay" Paula went to where she had the supplies and took out some water for her mother. "Mar I think we should rest here for a while we have time on our hands" Paula told her mother then she made a place for her to lie down.

Shana went for a look around just to see if she could see if Chad and Jake were anywhere near them. When she came back Monica wanted to talk to her. While Paula was fixing some food for them she called Shana to her "Shana I am not going to last very long in this world I would like you to promise me that you will take care of Paula?" Monica begged her.

Shana did not know quite what to say this was her chance to get rid of the both of them.

Monica looked straight into Shana's eyes "Oh that goes without asking you know I will do anything for you." Monica could rest now thinking that her daughter was going to be looked after

They walked around looking for some kind of a clue as to which way they went. "Hey Jake over here" Chad called he had found some foot prints in the soft dirt. "Yeah there are three set and look at this set they seem to be deeper than the others." Jake notice "this heavy ones look like they are made that way the other are normal" Chad said.

The men followed the tracks until it got dark and then they could not see the trail anymore.

The next day the women were up and off before day light they had to get to the next stop. The next stop was a small village was had

Quakers living there but had since left. Paula had arranged a house there for them some time ago.

Shana had left a sign for the men and she saw hopping they would catch up soon. She had to get rid of the and go in a different direction it was getting to late to make that kind of a move.

Monica called Paula up to her she wanted to talk. "Paula how much longer will it take before we stop. I don't think I can hang out much longer" "It won't be long now Mar and you will be able to rest for a long time."

The men had gotten to the cannon and all that was left was two horses and a cold fire. The poor horses look like they need water feed. "Jake I think it would be a good idea to take the horses with us we might need them" "Yeah I will get them some feed and water and the we can move on. Jake said. Chad walked around just to stretch the legs and he picked up a tassel from a jacket. "Jake are you ready to go I know which they went I found a piece of a jacket I saw Shana wear once. Now we know who is leaving us the clues." "Ah she is alive too well we can get the three of them in one net. If she think she can get out of this by informing on the other she sadly mistaken." Chad was starting to go.

Paula settled her mother down in the house she set up for her" You can rest mother I think I should send Shana back away s to make sure that no one has followed us.

Shana went back down the way they came for a bit but could not see Jake and Chad.

Suddenly she saw a flash it may be the shine on their guns Shana waved her hat as to give them the sign to come on in. She hurried back to the house and told Paula "Um it is safe no one is following" Shana smiled.

It was not long before the men got the house but they had to be careful. They remembered to many times they had been this close and it all went wrong.

This time they made sure they had the jump on them. "Jake you cover the back and I will go in. And jake let's not blow this time we won't get another chance like this." All was set up and Chad went in to the house. "Hi ladies you are all under arrest. Now just step forward but drop your guns on the floor first. Shana started for the back door but Jake was there." Going somewhere Shana? Back in there with the others. "How did you bastards catch up with us so fast"? Monica growled. "Ah Monica you have a snitch in your mist" Chad looked straight at Shana "you bitch Paula went to grab at Shana but Jake stoped her." Now ladies we wont have any of that we have a long way to go and I do not want to have to breaking you lot up all the way.

It was going to take three day of hard riding to get back to town and it was not go as smooth as they want it to. For one thing they forgot all about Shana and her knives.

It was late one night when they had to camp for the night. Chad had Monica tied up to a tree along with Paula. They thought it would be better to tie Shana up to another tree. Chad and Jake had to take turns watching them. But both men were so done in they feel asleep and that is when Shana struck. She managed to get one of her knifes out cut herself lose. Then she headed for Paula she had all most stuck the knife into Paula when Paula seen her and screamed. Jake jump up and shot the knife out of Shana's hand "Oh you blood bastard oh my hand" Shana screamed. Chad took his bandana from around his neck "Here now go and sit over there "Chad searched her for more weapons then tied her up again.

Jake mad sure that there were no more hidden weapons while he was searching Paula Monica called out "Get your hands of my daughter" "Don't worry you are next I know about you and your tricks old girl."

Having made sure that all the ladies were not concealing any weapons it was time to get some more rest.

The rest of the way back to town was all most clear of problems. There was a lot of talking and moaning from the ladies.

When they got back to town it was still early and not too many people were about. This gave them a chance to get the women into the jail safe.

But as soon as the people heard about the women were in the jail a crowd started to gather. "Hey you two that crowd is going to get ugly maybe you have better let us go" Monica called out.

Jake came into the cells "Monica you can stop your yelling you are not getting out of this. This time you are going straight to the gallows" Shana asked for a doctor. She all so want to talk to Chad. "Shut your mouth bitch you traitor. After all I did for you and where did you hide my money" Monica called out. "You are not getting your hands on that old woman" Shana went back to her cot.

Chad and Jake were sitting around they had to stay there make sure the angry mob outside did not get out of hand. "Jake this is going to get ugly here take this and we had better go out there." Chad handed him a rifle.

Once outside Chad held up his hands and said "There is no good trying to get to the women we are going to see that they stand trial. Now you had better go home." The most of the crowd left and went home but the trouble maker stayed.

The judge was due in town the next day and the men had to keep the trouble maker away. Chad thought it was a lot easer if he just locked the office up and wait till the judge came. But the trouble maker were not going away they had a belly full of whisky and keep on yelling "Let them out we have a nice strong rope here. You won't need the judge.

After a while it quieten down outside but this was all ways a bad sign. Chad went to the window open it a tad he could not see anyone around. Jake could smell smoke "Chad get some water quick they have set fire to the back door" They put that out but the door was badly damaged.

Jake took up the watch on the back door and Chad took up the watch on the front door. It seem to take forever but it started to get light now all had to do was hang out till the judge got there on the stage coach.

It was about noon when the judge stepped of the coach he went straight to the jail "Chad I heard you had some bad women in your jail" "Yes your honour these women have evading the law for some time now "Chad told him." Okay the we will set up court in the morning it is to late now we must get a jury together.

The next day the hotel bar was closed and the court room was set up. A Jury of twelve men heard all of the evidence. The judge said "now that you have heard all the evidence and have had time to consider you verdict. How do you fine guilty or not guilty." The foreman stood up and said "we fined that all three are guilty sir."

Then the court room erupted in to loud cheers the judge bang the gavel on the desk to make them stop. After he had control of the room he had to hand down the sentence "I have no choice but to sentence all the women to had by the neck until you die and may god have mercy on your souls"

Chad took the women back to the jail to wait for the carpenter to build the scaffold to have them hung by the neck. The next day when the building was finished Chad walked them up to the hanging nose. The nose was placed over their heads and made tight. The hangman then pulled the leaver.

The End